Sugar Plum
SCARY

WRITTEN BY
CIARAN MURTAGH

ILLUSTRATED BY
EMI ORDÁS

OXFOR
UNIVERSITY PR

OXFORD
UNIVERSITY PRESS

Great Clarendon Street, Oxford, OX2 6DP, United Kingdom

Oxford University Press is a department of the University of Oxford. It furthers the University's objective of excellence in research, scholarship, and education by publishing worldwide. Oxford is a registered trade mark of Oxford University Press in the UK and in certain other countries

Text © Ciaran Murtagh 2015
Illustrations © Emi Ordás 2015

The moral rights of the author have been asserted

First published 2015
This edition published 2019

British Library Cataloguing in Publication Data
Data available

ISBN: 978-0-19-276974-9

10 9 8 7 6 5 4 3 2 1

Paper used in the production of this book is a natural, recyclable product made from wood grown in sustainable forests. The manufacturing process conforms to the environmental regulations of the country of origin.

Printed in China

Acknowledgements
Series Advisor: Nikki Gamble

Helping your child to read

Before they start

- Talk about the back cover blurb. What does your child know about tooth fairies? How might Sugar Plum be different?

- Look at the front cover. What kind of story does your child think this will be? Do they think Sugar Plum looks nice or scary?

During reading

- Let your child read at their own pace – don't worry if it's slow. They could read silently, or read to you out loud.

- Help them to work out words they don't know by saying each sound out loud and then blending them to say the word, e.g. *f-l-oor-b-oar-d-s, floorboards.*

- If your child still struggles with a word, just tell them the word and move on.

- Give them lots of praise for good reading!

After reading

- Look at pages 36 to 39 for some fun activities.

Introduction

What do you and your friends do
when your baby teeth fall out?
All around the world, children
do different things with their
baby teeth. In some countries,
children throw their baby teeth
up at the sun, or hide them
under the floorboards. And in
Spain children often leave their
teeth for the tooth mouse! But in
many countries round the world,
children leave their teeth for
the tooth fairy – and the tooth
fairy gives them a coin for
each tooth.

Chapter One

Sugar Plum the tooth fairy flew into the bedroom and landed on the carpet. Her best friend, Lemonade, watched from the window sill.

"Go on," whispered Lemonade. "Get the tooth!"

Sugar Plum was a very clumsy tooth fairy. She tried her best to be quiet, but she found it hard. Things always went wrong when she tried to collect children's teeth. But this time, she was going to get it right! She flew towards the bed.

Sugar Plum banged into the bedside table.

The boy in the
bed rolled over, but
he was still asleep.

Sugar Plum took off again …

... and landed on a teddy bear's tummy.

Squeak!

Sugar Plum held her breath but the boy kept snoring.

Double phew!

Sugar Plum stuck her arm under the pillow and found the tooth. She pulled it out and waved it at Lemonade. "Got it!" she grinned.

Just then, a speck of dust tickled Sugar Plum's nose. She sneezed an **enormous** sneeze.

The boy woke up and screamed in surprise.

A-a-a-achoooooooo!

Sugar Plum dropped the tooth and flew out of the window. Lemonade followed. They didn't look back.

"Was that better than last time?" asked Sugar Plum.

Lemonade shook his head.

"It was worse!" he thought.

Chapter Two

Bottletop was the leader of the tooth fairies, and he wasn't pleased. "That was a disaster!" he said. "This isn't the first time, is it, Sugar Plum?"

Sugar Plum shook her head.

"There was the time you dropped the tooth down a drain …

Oops!

... the time you fell through a cat flap ...

Hiss!

... and the time you scared
a girl so much she ran into a
wardrobe – without opening
it first!"

"Next time I'll be
better," said Sugar Plum.

"I'm afraid there won't be a next time," said Bottletop. "Not everyone can be a tooth-collecting fairy, Sugar Plum. I found it very difficult myself.

One of my wings is smaller than the other, so I always fly in circles."

Bottletop shook his head. "It was a disaster!" he said. "But I found a job I was good at, and you will too."

"I'll help!" said Lemonade.

Sugar Plum smiled. She was glad to have someone so kind as her best friend.

"Good," said Bottletop. "We'll find the right job for Sugar Plum and all live *happily* ever after."

Chapter Three

"I really wanted to be a tooth-collecting fairy," said Sugar Plum. "But I'm terrible at it!"

"I've been telling you that for years," said Verruca nastily. "You're more *scary* than *fairy*. That's what I'm going to call you from now on: Sugar Plum Scary!"

Lemonade gave Verruca an angry look.

Verruca was always mean to Sugar Plum.

"Don't worry, Sugar Plum," Lemonade said.

"We'll find the right job for you, I'm sure of it!"

For the next few days, Lemonade tried to find Sugar Plum a job. There was: Chief Wing Sparkler …

Disaster!

Tooth Polisher …

Double disaster!

Fairy Dust Collector ...

COUGH!

Triple disaster!

By the end of the week, Sugar Plum was more upset than ever. None of her new jobs had worked out.

Chapter Four

The next morning, Sugar Plum
packed all of her things into a
nutshell case.

"Where are you going
to go?" asked Lemonade.

Sugar Plum shrugged.
"I don't know," she said.

"But there aren't any jobs I can do here."

Suddenly, they heard a loud cry. It was coming from Bottletop's room.

Aaaaaaaah!

The two fairies raced to see what had happened.

They found Bottletop flapping around in
circles and Verruca trying to calm him down.
"They've all gone!" cried Bottletop.
"What's all gone?" asked Sugar Plum.

Bottletop led the fairies
down a staircase
to a safe.

It was where the fairies kept
their coins. They needed those
coins to swap for teeth!

The safe was  empty.

"Our coins," groaned Bottletop.
"They've gone!"

Bottletop was very worried.

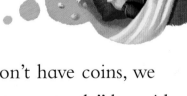

"If we don't have coins, we
can't collect any teeth," he said.
"And if we can't collect
any teeth – what will
happen then?"

"There must be more coins somewhere!" said Lemonade.

"Well, there is a super-secret store," said Bottletop. He showed them a hidden safe behind a picture. "But that's only for emergencies."

"This *is* an emergency," said Lemonade.

"But what if the robbers come back?"
asked Bottletop.

"I'll guard the safe," said Sugar Plum bravely.

Verruca laughed. "No you won't," she said.
"This is a job for a real fairy! *I'll* be
the guard."

And so, that night, Verruca guarded the coins.

Chapter Five

Sugar Plum was fast asleep when she heard the cry.

Help! Help!

She leaped out of bed to see what was happening.

Lemonade rushed out of his bedroom too. They dashed to the secret safe.

Verruca was racing the other way!

"The robbers are back. Hide!" she shouted.

"Lemonade! Quick! We need to stop the robbers!" said Sugar Plum.

Bravely, the two friends flew down the staircase.

It was dark at the bottom of the stairs.

"Who's there?" said Sugar Plum, as bravely as she could.

"Go away," said a gruff voice.

Sugar Plum marched on. She turned a corner and gasped at what she saw. A troll was putting the fairies' coins into a sack.

"Stop that!" said Sugar Plum. "Or you'll be sorry!"

The troll laughed.

"I'm not scared of a pretty, pinky, twinkly fairy," he growled.

"But I'm not a pretty, pinky, twinkly fairy," said Sugar Plum. "I'm Sugar Plum Scary, the scariest fairy of them all!"

Just then a speck of dust landed on Sugar Plum's nose.

Sugar Plum sneezed – very loudly.

The walls wobbled and the ground shook.
The troll dropped his sack and ran away with
his hands over his ears. He never looked back.

Chapter Six

The next morning, there was a grand ceremony.
Bottletop gave Sugar Plum a green sash
saying 'Chief Fairy Guard'. Sugar Plum
beamed with pride.

"Well done, Sugar Plum!" said Bottletop.
"Thanks to you, tooth fairies can collect teeth
again. You are a brilliant Fairy Guard!"
Everyone clapped,
even Verruca.

From that day on, nothing stopped the fairies from collecting teeth and leaving coins. All thanks to the clumsiest and bravest fairy of them all:

Sugar Plum SCARY

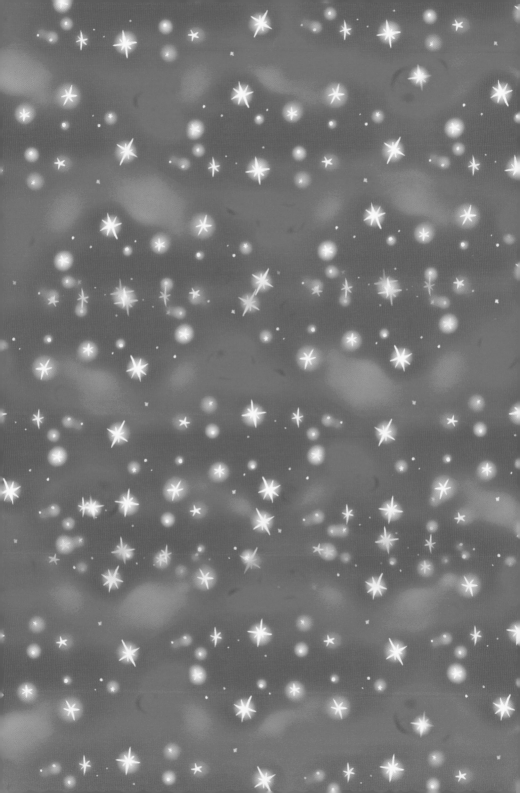

After reading activities

Quick quiz

See how fast you can answer these questions!
Look back at the story if you can't remember.

1) What was Sugar Plum's best friend's name?

2) What made the boy wake up when Sugar Plum was taking his tooth?

3) Why did Bottletop think Sugar Plum couldn't be a tooth-collecting fairy?

4) What kind of person was Verruca at the start of the story?

5) What happened when Sugar Plum tried to be a tooth polisher?

6) Why did Bottletop get upset?

7) How did Sugar Plum's sneezing help to defeat the troll?

8) What job did Sugar Plum get in the end?

Answers: 1) Lemonade; **2)** Sugar Plum sneezed loudly; **3)** she was too clumsy and things kept going wrong; **4)** she was unkind to Sugar Plum and called her names; **5)** it was a disaster – she whacked Bottletop on the head; **6)** someone had stolen some of the fairies' coins; **7)** she made such a loud noise that he ran away; **8)** Chief Fairy Guard.

Talk about it!

- Was Lemonade a good friend to Sugar Plum? What did he do to help her?

- If you were a fairy, would you like to be a tooth collector, wing sparkler, tooth polisher or fairy guard? Why?

- Do you think Verruca changed her mind about Sugar Plum at the end of the story? Can you find a clue about this on page 33?

Try this!

Next time you lose a tooth, write a note and draw a picture for the tooth fairy. Slip it under your pillow with the tooth. What will your note say?

Make up your own fairy

Look at the fairies below and give them all names. Are they friendly or nasty? What kind of jobs do they do? What kind of foods do they like? You can decide!

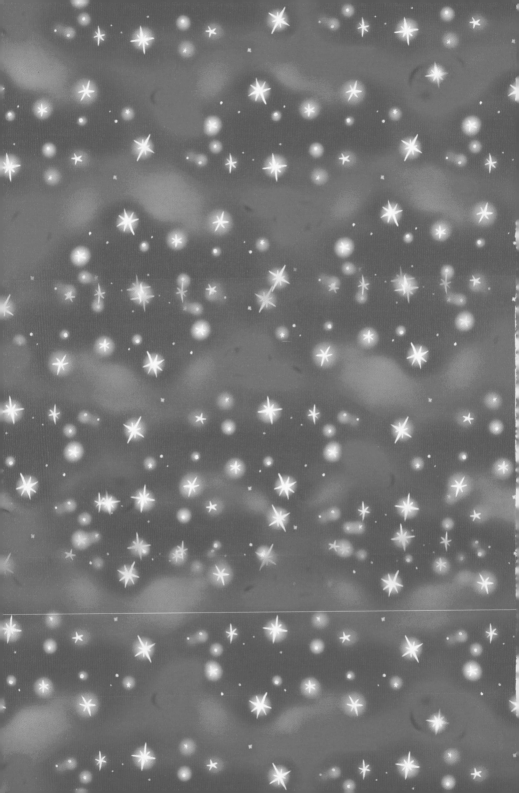